MURDERS

MD. ADEEL ASHRAF

This novel is dedicated to those who have inspired me. To those who have shared their wisdom, their stories, and their love. To those who have made me laugh, dream, and see the world with greater clarity. To those who have shown me that strength comes in all shapes, sizes, and forms. Thank you for your passion and kind hearts. You are the reason I am here and I thank you for your invaluable lessons.

Contents

Acknowledgements

I would like to extend my sincerest gratitude to everyone who has been involved in the creation of this novel. From the authors who crafted the story, to the editors who polished the text, to the cover artists who brought the book to life, everyone involved has my utmost respect and admiration.

The journey to bring this novel to the world has been long and challenging, and without the teamwork of all these incredible individuals, it would not have been possible. Your dedication and hard work have been invaluable, and I am truly grateful to have been part of the process. Thank you!

CHAPTER ONE

Ceder Creek

The sun was setting on the small suburban town of Cedar Creek. The streets were empty and quiet, but there was an eerie stillness in the air that seemed to echo the recent disappearance of high school student, James Archer.

Detective Smith had been on the case for weeks, and she was beginning to grow frustrated with the lack of progress. She had no leads and no clues to follow, so she had begun to dig deeper into the life of the missing teen. However, the more she investigated, the more she uncovered a sinister truth.

The evidence began to point to a murder-for-hire scheme, one that seemed to go all the way to the highest levels of the town's political and social elite. Detective Smith knew that she had to act fast if she were to save James' life.

She soon discovered that the murder plot was being orchestrated by a powerful and influential figure in town. With the help of her partner, Detective Jones, Smith worked to unravel the mystery and put an end to the conspiracy.

Finally, the duo was able to track down the mastermind behind the crimes and the killer who had taken James Archer. But the investigation didn't end there. Smith and Jones soon uncovered a web of lies and deceit that stretched far beyond the initial case, revealing a much larger evil lurking beneath the surface of the small town.

In the end, justice was served, and the killer was brought to justice. But the memory of James Archer and the secrets of Cedar Creek still remain.

CHAPTER TWO

Willow Creek

Once upon a time, in a small town named Willow Creek, a murder took place that sent shockwaves through the entire community. It all began on a peaceful autumn evening when the town's wealthiest and most powerful resident, Mr. Harrison, was found dead in his study with a bullet wound to the head.

Detective John, who was assigned to the case, immediately started his investigation. He talked to the staff and other members of the family but nobody had any idea of who could have committed such a heinous crime.

The next day, the will of Mr. Harrison was read, and it was revealed that his entire fortune was to be inherited by his youngest daughter, Ashley. This caused quite a stir in the town as many people had a motive for murder, including Ashley's siblings and their spouses who were suddenly cut off from their expected inheritance.

Detective John delved deeper into the case and found out that Ashley had a troubled past and was known to have a drug addiction. He also learned that Ashley had been in a heated argument with her father the day before he was murdered.

However, the real twist in the case came when the gun that was used to kill Mr. Harrison was found in the possession of his personal driver, who had been missing since the night of the murder. The driver had a solid alibi and claimed that Ashley had planted the gun on him in a desperate attempt to frame him.

The final piece of the puzzle was solved when Ashley broke down and confessed to the murder. She had gone to confront her father about her drug addiction and the financial support she needed to overcome it. But their argument escalated, and in a fit of rage, she had taken the gun from her father's desk and shot him.

In the end, justice was served, and Ashley was sentenced to life in prison for the murder of

Mr. Harrison. The small town of Willow Creek slowly went back to its peaceful existence, but the shocking events of that autumn evening would never be forgotten.

CHAPTER THREE

Blackwood

In the quiet town of Blackwood, a series of mysterious deaths had the residents on edge. All of the victims were high-profile individuals and their deaths were made to look like accidents or suicides.

Detective Emma was called in to investigate the case and found a strange pattern in the way the victims were killed. She soon realized that the murders were linked to a secret society, known as the "Shadow Order," that operated in the town.

The Shadow Order was a group of wealthy and influential individuals who pulled the strings behind the scenes and controlled the town. Detective Emma started to dig deeper and found out that the latest string of murders was carried out to eliminate those who posed a threat to the society's power and secrets.

One of the members of the Shadow Order, a well-known businessman named Mr. Collins, was the prime suspect. He was caught on camera near the scene of one of the murders, and his alibi was full of holes.

However, just when Detective Emma thought she had solved the case, she received a mysterious note that warned her to back off, or she would become the next victim. She didn't let the threat stop her and continued her investigation.

The final piece of the puzzle fell into place when Detective Emma discovered that the real mastermind behind the murders was the town's mayor, who was also the leader of the Shadow Order. The mayor was trying to consolidate his power and eliminate anyone who posed a threat to his authority.

In the end, Detective Emma put an end to the Shadow Order and brought the mayor to justice. The residents of Blackwood finally breathed a sigh of relief, but the mysterious events of those dark days would never be forgotten

Riverrdale

In the small town of Riverdale, a string of burglaries had left the residents feeling uneasy. The burglaries seemed to be random, but the common factor was that only high-value items were taken.

Detective Alex was assigned to the case and quickly realized that this was not a typical burglary case. He found that all of the burglaries had taken place in homes owned by members of a secret society, known as the "Elite Circle." The Elite Circle was a group of wealthy individuals who used their influence to control the town.

Detective Alex delved deeper into the case and found out that the burglaries were committed by a former member of the Elite Circle, who had been kicked out of the society and was now seeking revenge. The former member had inside information about the society and was using it to target their homes.

However, things took a turn for the worse when one of the members of the Elite Circle was found dead in their home, and the police had no leads. Detective Alex was certain that the death was related to the burglaries and that the murderer was someone from within the Elite Circle.

The final piece of the puzzle was solved when Detective Alex found out that the murderer was the society's leader, who had killed the member to cover up their involvement in the burglaries. The leader had taken the high-value items to fund their lavish lifestyle and was trying to silence anyone who posed a threat to their secret.

In the end, Detective Alex brought the murderer to justice, and the residents of Riverdale could finally sleep soundly at night. The mysterious events of those dark days would never be forgotten, and the Elite Circle was no more.

CHAPTER FIVE

Willow Creek Once again

It was a dark and stormy night in the small town of Willow Creek. Detective Jameson was on the case of a murder that had rocked the town. The victim, wealthy businessman Mr. Smith, had been found dead in his mansion with a knife plunged into his chest.

Detective Jameson immediately suspected Smith's wife, Mrs. Smith, who had a history of infidelity and arguments with her husband. However, when he questioned her, she had a solid alibi, having been at a charity event at the time of the murder.

Next, the detective turned to Smith's business partner, Mr. Green, who had recently been at odds with Smith over a business deal gone wrong. Green, too, had an alibi, having been in a meeting with several other people at the time of the murder.

Frustrated with the lack of leads, Detective Jameson decided to delve deeper into the victim's personal life. He discovered that Mr. Smith had a mistress, a young woman named Miss Rose, who was seen leaving the mansion on the night of the murder in a hurry.

Miss Rose was brought in for questioning, and at first, she claimed to know nothing about the murder. However, after hours of intense questioning, she finally broke down and confessed to killing Mr. Smith in a fit of jealousy and rage after he told her he was ending their affair.

With the murderer finally behind bars, Detective Jameson could close the case and bring a sense of justice to the town of Willow Creek. But, he couldn't shake the feeling that there was more to this case than met the eye. He vowed to continue his investigation until he uncovered the truth, no matter how long it took.

CHAPTER SIX

Maple Grove

It was a cold and blustery night in the small town of Maple Grove. The moon shone brightly in the night sky, casting an eerie glow across the deserted streets.

Detective Sam Smith had been called in to investigate a murder. The victim was a young woman named Sarah Miller, who had been discovered dead in her apartment. The coroner's report showed that she had been brutally stabbed multiple times with a sharp object.

Sam had been following leads all day, but he was no closer to solving the case. He had interviewed neighbors and searched the area, but nothing had turned up. As the hours passed, he began to feel as though he was going in circles.

Then, suddenly, an idea came to him. He remembered that Sarah had been seen talking to a mysterious stranger in the park a few nights before her death. It seemed like a longshot, but Sam decided to investigate further.

He tracked down the stranger and soon discovered that he was an ex-convict who had recently been released from prison. Sam arrested him and interrogated him, but the man denied any involvement in the murder.

Sam wasn't convinced and decided to look for more evidence. He combed through Sarah's apartment, looking for any clues that might point to the killer. After hours of searching, he finally found a clue: a small, bloody handkerchief tucked away in a drawer.

The handkerchief had the initial "J" embroidered on it. Sam realized that the killer must have left it behind. He ran a background check on the mysterious stranger and found out that his name was Johnny Jones.

Sam quickly connected the dots and realized that Johnny was the murderer. He arrested him and brought him to justice. Sarah's murder was solved, and the town of Maple Grove could rest easy.

CHAPTER SEVEN

Longford

The small town of Longford had seen its fair share of crime, but nothing quite like this. It had been only a few weeks since the body of prominent businessman Thomas Stanley had been found in his office, dead from a single gunshot wound to the head.

The police had ruled it a suicide but something felt off. His colleagues and family weren't convinced, but the police didn't have any leads. That was, until a mysterious figure called Larry showed up at the police station with a wild story.

According to Larry, he had seen Stanley and another man arguing in Stanley's office the night before Stanley died. Larry had watched from the shadows as the other man pulled a gun and shot Stanley. Larry had then fled the scene but kept an eye on the man as he fled town the following day.

Stanley's family and colleagues hired a private investigator to track down the mysterious man while the police continued to investigate. The PI followed the man to an abandoned house outside of town and discovered a trove of evidence, including the gun used to kill Stanley.

The man was arrested, and it was discovered he had ties to a powerful mob boss in the city. In exchange for his release, the mob boss agreed to provide information on other crimes.

The case was officially closed, and the family was able to find peace after the tragedy. But for the citizens of Longford, the crime remained a mystery. Who was the mysterious man, and what was his motive? Was it all part of a larger, sinister plot?

CHAPTER EIGHT

Blackridge

It was a cold, dark night in the small town of Blackridge. The streets were deserted and an eerie silence hung in the air. Detective Mason was on the case. He had been called to investigate a strange murder.

The victim was a young woman named Anna Chambers. She had been found in her apartment, brutally murdered. Her body had been brutally beaten and there were signs of strangulation. There were no signs of robbery and no clues left at the scene.

Detective Mason had very little to go on. He began interviewing the people in Anna's apartment building. He was able to gather some information, but it seemed that nobody had seen or heard anything suspicious.

The detective decided to look into other leads. He obtained a list of people who had a connection to the victim. He started talking to them, searching for anyone who had a motive or might have had access to the apartment.

He soon found a suspect, a man by the name of Michael Carter. He had a prior criminal record and had recently argued with Anna. Detective Mason decided to bring him in for questioning.

During the interrogation, Michael broke down and confessed to the murder. He claimed that he had gone to Anna's apartment that night to talk to her, but they had ended up fighting. Michael had become enraged and attacked her.

Detective Mason arrested Michael and charged him with murder. He was sentenced to life in prison.

The Mystery Man

It was a dark and stormy night, and the clock had just struck midnight. The wind howled outside, and thunder rumbled through the night sky. Inside, the lights were all off, but the detective was still awake, pacing around the living room, his eyes scanning the scene of the crime.

He had been summoned by the local police to investigate a mysterious murder. It had been a gruesome killing, with the body of a young woman found in a nearby alley. Nobody could seem to figure out what had happened, or who had done it.

The detective glanced around the room. Everything seemed to be in order. All the items in the room were as they should be; there was no sign of a struggle.

He followed a faint trail of blood that had been left behind. It led him upstairs, to a bedroom. He could tell something serious had happened in this room; the furniture had been overturned and there were signs of a struggle.

He examined the room carefully, searching for any clues that might help him solve the case. He noticed a small piece of paper on the dresser. It was a letter addressed to the victim, from someone called 'The Hangman'.

The detective studied the letter carefully. It seemed to be a chilling message of retribution. Whoever this 'Hangman' was, they had killed the victim as a warning to others.

He quickly alerted the police and they began an immediate investigation. After a few days, they had a suspect in custody. The suspect was a man named John Smith, who had a long criminal history.

The detective grilled Smith, who eventually confessed to the crime. He said he had been hired by 'The Hangman' to kill the victim. He had no idea who The Hangman was or why he had been hired.

The detective soon discovered that The Hangman was a mysterious figure who had been exacting revenge on those he deemed worthy of it. The Hangman was never seen and never caught.

The case was never solved and The Hangman was never found. He remains a mysterious figure to this day.

CHAPTER TEN

Neighbour

It was a dark and stormy night, and Detective John Smith was on the case. He had been called to investigate a suspicious death on the outskirts of town. When he arrived, he found the body of a young woman. She had been brutally murdered and her body showed signs of a violent struggle.

John quickly surmised that the woman had been killed by someone she knew. There were no signs of forced entry, so it appeared the killer was someone she was familiar with.

John began to investigate further, interviewing family and friends of the victim. Each person he talked to had a different story about the night of the murder. Some said they had seen her alive and well just hours before she was found dead. Others said they saw her arguing with someone just minutes before her death.

John also found that the woman had several enemies. She had recently been in a heated dispute with her neighbor over noise levels, which could have provided a motive for murder. She had also received numerous death threats from an unknown source in the months leading up to her death.

John was determined to find the killer and began to piece the clues together. He soon came to the conclusion that the victim had been killed by her neighbor in a fit of rage. John confronted the neighbor and he quickly confessed to the crime.

With the killer in custody, the mystery was solved and justice was served. Detective John Smith had solved the case and brought closure to the victim's family.